What does Daddy do?

Rachel Bright

PUFFIN

This is
DaiSy.

Every day except Wednesday,
Daisy's daddy takes her to
LITTLE NIPPERS NURSERY
before he goes to work.
At 8 o'clock, he calls upstairs,
"Are you ready, Princess?
Time to go!"
And Daisy calls back,
"Yes, Daddy,
LET'S GO!"

They climb into the car
and Daddy says, "All safe and belted-up?"
And Daisy says, "Yes, Daddy,

LET'S GO!"

And in a go-when-the-lights-are-green

vrOOOM of the engine

they get to nursery
in no time at all.

Then, after a
big cuddle,
Daisy waves goodbye
until Daddy's car
disappears round
the corner . . .

LITTLE
NIPPERS
NURSERY

and for just a little bit longer after that.

At nursery, Daisy has three best friends:
Dexter, Evie and Bob.
They always play together and talk
about **important** things they know.

One Tuesday, when they
were building a **giant** sandcastle,
DeXter suddenly stOod up and
in a very **lOud** voice said,
"Did you knOw . . .

PLAY NICELY
IN THE SANDPIT

NO
BEING
MEAN

NO
BURYING

NO
BEING
MEAN

NO
THROWING SAND
ABOUT THE PLACE

"...My daddy is a **fireman!**
He has a big red truck
with a round-and-round light.
It goes Nee Nar
Nee Nar
Nee Nar!
He squirts water at
fires and rescues
people and
sometimes
kittens!"

"Well," said Evie,
"my daddy is a
doctOr!
He maKes sicky peOple better
and he listens tO their hearts go
BOOM BOOM
and he has
fOurteen
pencils
in a tub."

And then BOb said, "Well, my daddy is a **teacher!** He maKes children very clever and he knOws **eVerything** abOut **eVerything**, *especially* **volcanOes**."

MOLTEN LAVA

BIG BOOK OF VOLCANO

VOLCANO COLOURING IN

THE LITTLE BOOK OF BIG VOLCANOES

"Does he?" said Daisy.
"Yes," said Bob.
"He does.

What does **your daddy** do?"
"Hmmm," thought Daisy.
"What *does* Daddy **do?**"

Daisy knew that Daddy left in the mOrning in a **smart stripey suit** . . .

. . . wearing **nice shiny** shOes that gO **click** on the floOr.

And he
always took his
special case –
the one that
pops open
when the **secret**
numbers match.

And she knew he came back at five twenty-five to pick her up

and say "Hello, sweetheart, have you had a nice day?"

BUT...
What about
all the **time**
in-between?

"What dOes Daddy dO?"
thOught DaiSy.

"What dOes Daddy dO?"

And then she remembered . . .

"My daddy is an eXplorer!" said Daisy.

"Is he?" said Evie.
"Yes, he is!" said Daisy.
"He climbs to the
highest of high-up places
because he has
mountains
of paperwork to get
on top of."

VERY SAFE
SAFETY
ROPE

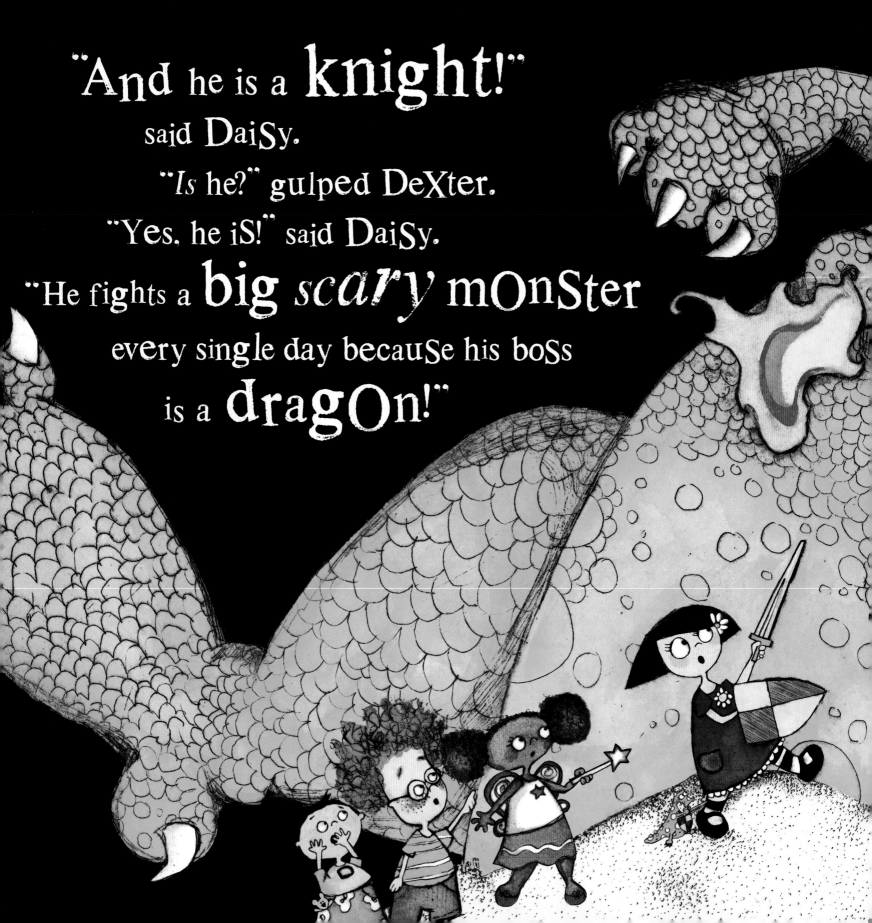

"And he is a **knight!**" said Daisy.

"*Is he?*" gulped Dexter.

"Yes, he is!" said Daisy.

"He fights a **big** *scary* **mOnSter** every single day because his boss is a **dragOn!**"

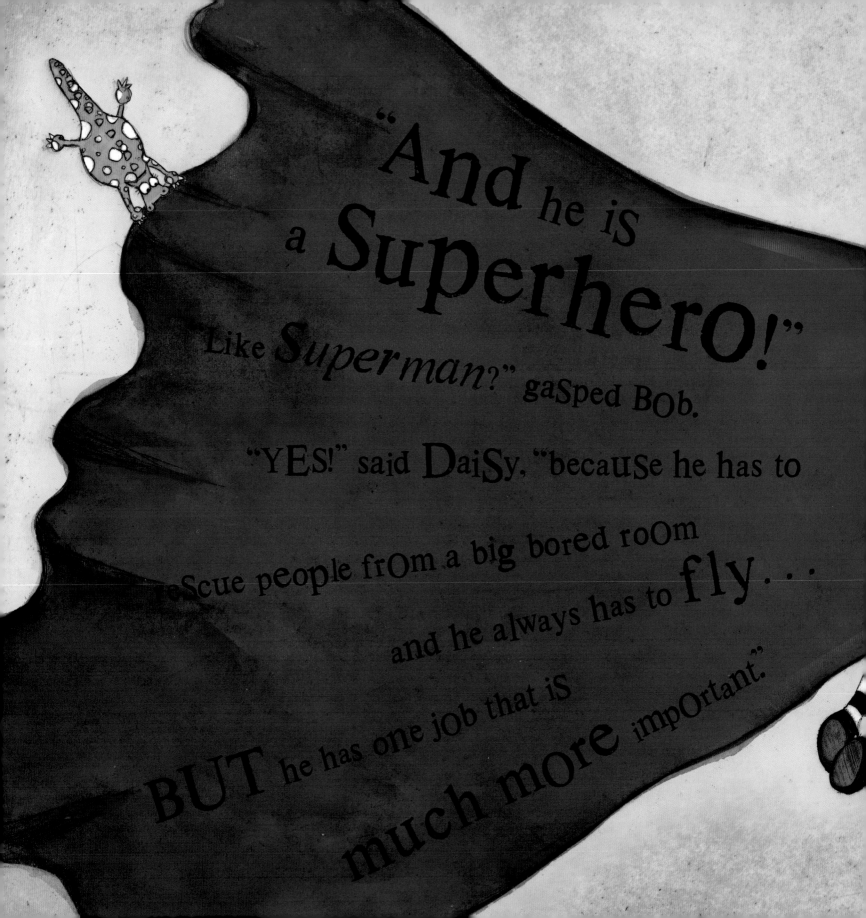

"And he is a Superhero!"

"Like Superman?" gasped Bob.

"YES!" said Daisy, "because he has to rescue people from a big bored room and he always has to fly...

BUT he has one job that is much more important."

"But **what's** mOre impOrtant than being an

EXPLORERSUPERKNIGHT?"

said Evie
and DeXter
and BOb.

"Well," said Daisy, "he is my **daddy!**

And **that** is what
he **dOes**."

I ♥
YOU DADDY

FOr my **mummy** and **daddy**,

whO went on adVentureS everyday,

sO I cOuld belieVe anything is pOsSible

With big, huge thanks to SchminckE and all
the incredible peOple who madE this bOok pOsSible

PUFFIN BOOKS
Published by the Penguin Group: London. New York. Australia.
Canada. India. Ireland. New Zealand and South Africa
Penguin Books Ltd.
Registered Offices: 80 Strand. London WC2R 0RL. England
puffinbooks.com
First published by Puffin Books 2009
5 7 9 10 8 6 4

Printed in China
ISBN: 978–0–141–50264–9

I ❤ YOU DADDY